If You Ever Lose Hope...

Jordana Chana Mayim

MOSAIC
STREET
PRESS

To get in touch with the publisher, please email us at hello@mosaicstreetpress.com 
To get in touch with the author, please email her at jordanamayim@yahoo.com

Book designers: Jordana Chana Mayim and Merion Art and Repro Center
Editor: Mario Monterrubio Gañán
Proofreader: Rachel Small
Mosaic Street Press logo designer: ÂGrizon

An extra special thank-you to Ellen for her tremendous generosity and for giving an artist two of the most exquisite things that one can give: the time and the space to be FREE to CREATE.

The illustrations are collages made from photographs that Jordana took during her travels. To learn more about the illustrations and her travels, please visit https://www.jordanamayim.com/hope-illustrations

First Edition

Publisher's Cataloging-in-Publication Data
Names: Mayim, Jordana Chana, author, illustrator.
Title: If you ever lose hope... / Jordana Chana Mayim.
Description: Narberth, PA : Mosaic Street Press, 2021. | Summary: To regain hope, a woman follows the advice of those who've endured injustice and
    anguish and felt joy again.
Identifiers: LCCN 2020922988 (print) | ISBN 978-1-948267-08-3 (paperback) | ISBN 978-1-948267-09-0 (hardcover) | ISBN 978-1-948267-10-6 (ebook)
Subjects: LCSH: Young adult fiction. | Illustrated works. | CYAC: Determination (Personality trait)--Fiction. | Hope--Fiction. | Depression--Fiction. |
    BISAC: YOUNG ADULT FICTION / Girls & Women. | YOUNG ADULT FICTION / Social Themes / Depression. | YOUNG ADULT FICTION /
    Social Themes / Self-Esteem & Self-Reliance.
Classification: LCC PZ7.1.M39 If 2021 (print) | LCC PZ7.1.M39 (ebook) | DDC [Fic]--dc23.

To Andrea
for being a garden,
a sun,
and a savior

and

To the Survivors,
for rising from the ashes,
for standing,
for soaring,
for teaching:
There is a reason why.
Carry on.

$$\text{One day...}$$

One day...

...she lost hope.

She looked for it in the darkness
that now enveloped her.

She could not find it.

Many things, however,
emerged from the shadows
and found their way to her.

Ugly things.

Painful things.

Injustice stormed in, thundering,

"WHAT HAS BEEN WILL ALWAYS BE!"

Sorrow sank into her soul and vowed,
in a voice

as quiet as tears that drown,

"I will *never* leave you."

Fear arrived

invisible,

impalpable,

and staked its claim to
all her thoughts and feelings
as it whispered,

"Mine.

Mine.

Mine."

But there were also other voices.
Other words.
Gifts from the Survivors.

The Survivors—

those who had met the whiplash of
"I will break you"
with an indomitable:

"STANDING!"

those who had defied the flames of
"Destroyed forever"
with a blazing:

"UP FROM THE ASHES!"

those who had followed the commands of
their capsized boats:

"Swim until you reach the shore...

...and then

Soar!"

—they had crossed paths with her.
Each Survivor had planted words of hope within her,
and through repetition,
ensured that their messages took root
for when, not if,
she needed those words.

Survivors know there is always a "when."

But not wanting to scare her, they always spoke "if."

"If you ever lose hope,"
one Survivor had told her,
"retrace your steps.
Find the moment you last had it.
Take it with you."

In her mind she journeyed to a place
that her feet could not carry her: the past.

She found the last moment the sun had blazed
not above her but within her,
and raised towards its golden beams
all that remained of her light:
an extinguished candle.

"Kindle a fire that will guide me in the present
and illuminate a path to the future,"
she pleaded.

Orange flames consumed wick and wax instantaneously,
then shed milk-white tears as their glow dimmed
and their voices all but failed them.

"We're sorry. We're not coming with you."

"If you ever lose hope,"
another Survivor had told her,
"continue to put one foot in front of the other.
As you walk,
you will find that hope walks towards you."

She walked.
She did not get far:
a wall was before her.

Polished stones,
as slippery as glass and embedded in cement,
watched her step backwards.

She asked, "How can I—"

A single stone attempted to answer, "You can—"
but the wall buried both question and response
with a booming,

"YOU CANNOT.
I CANNOT BE CLIMBED."

Her fingers scoured the wall's surface for
what her eyes might miss:
a place to put a foot, a hand,
the possibility of going forward.

      Nothing.

          Her eyes gazed upwards
          to where her hands could not reach.

                    She saw no end to the stones.

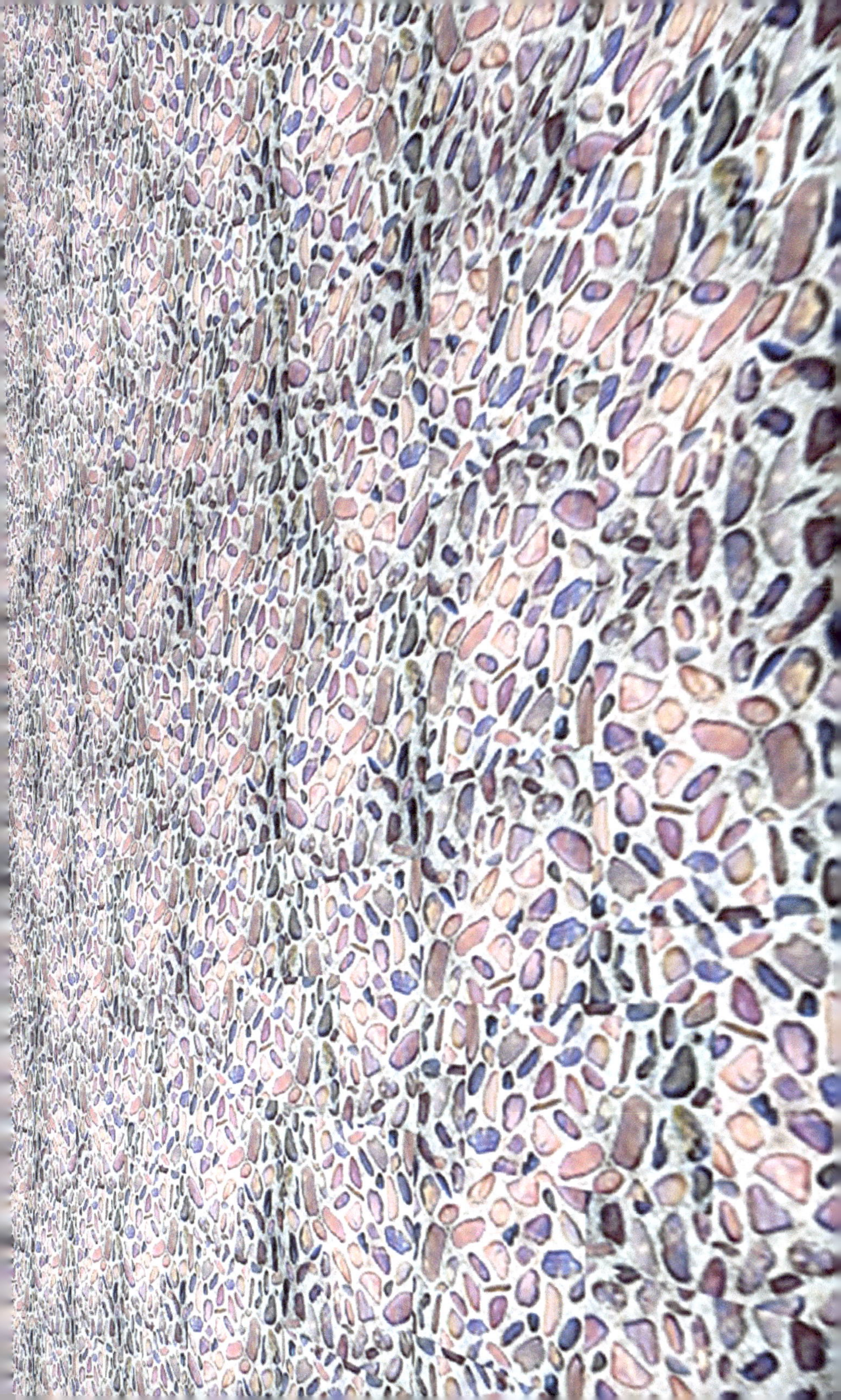

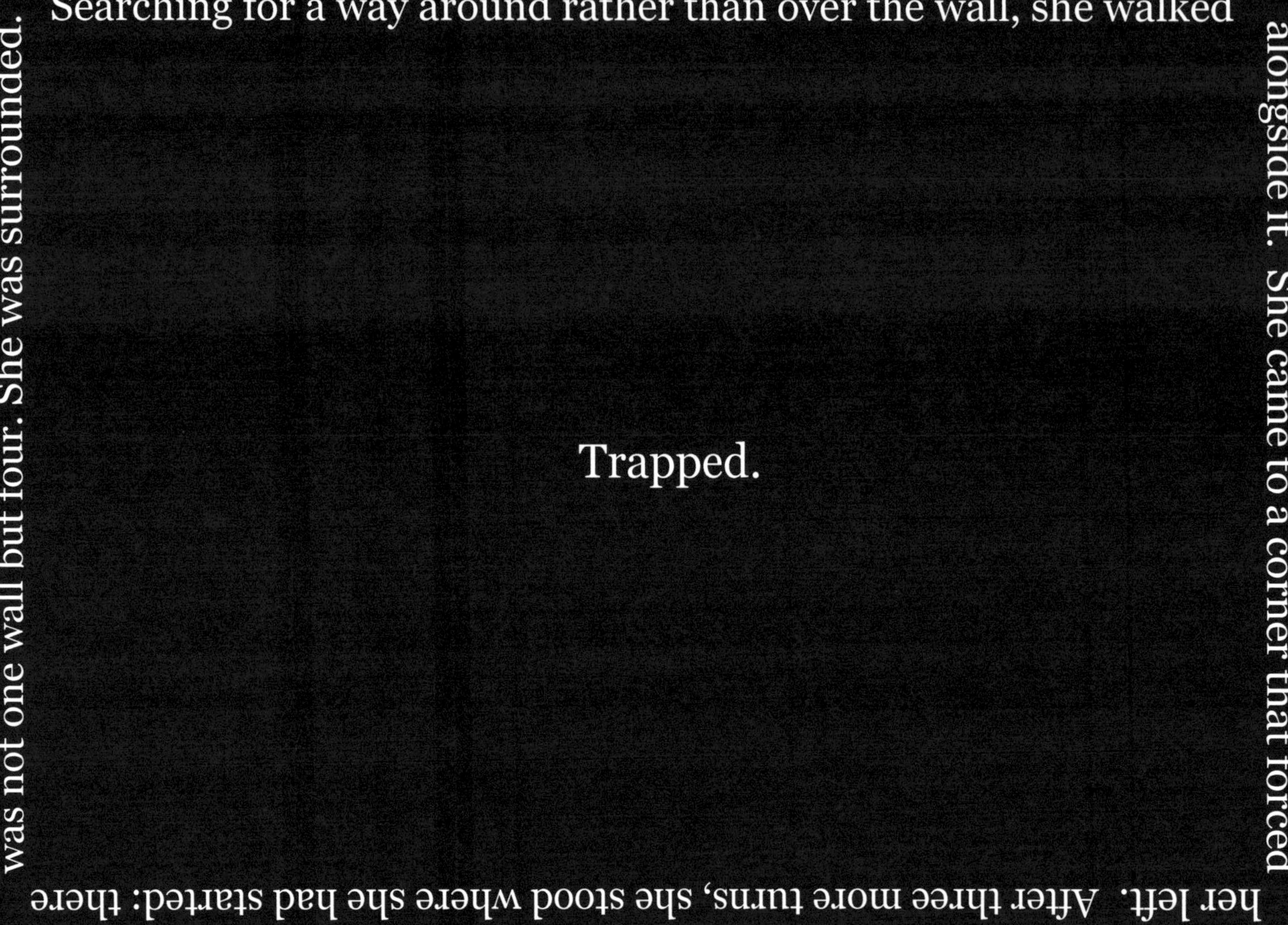

Searching for a way around rather than over the wall, she walked
alongside it. She came to a corner that forced
her left. After three more turns, she stood where she had started: there
was not one wall but four. She was surrounded.

Trapped.

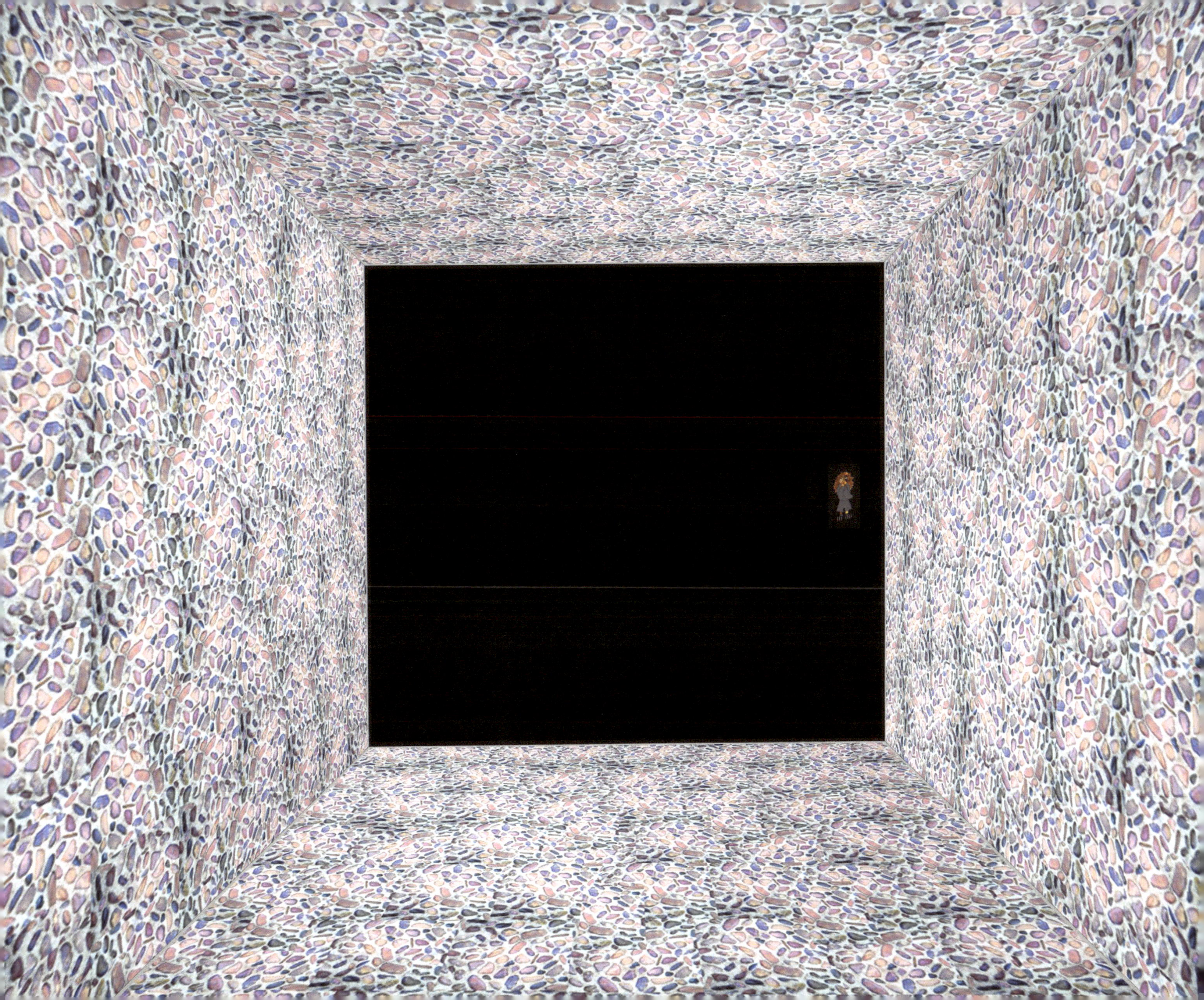

Nonetheless, she heeded the Survivor's words
and continued to put
                    one foot
                            in front of
                                    the other.

        She tread the circular path of the imprisoned,
    and her mind soon mirrored the movement of her feet;
            her thoughts were reduced to

                                            cages
                                without
            keys.

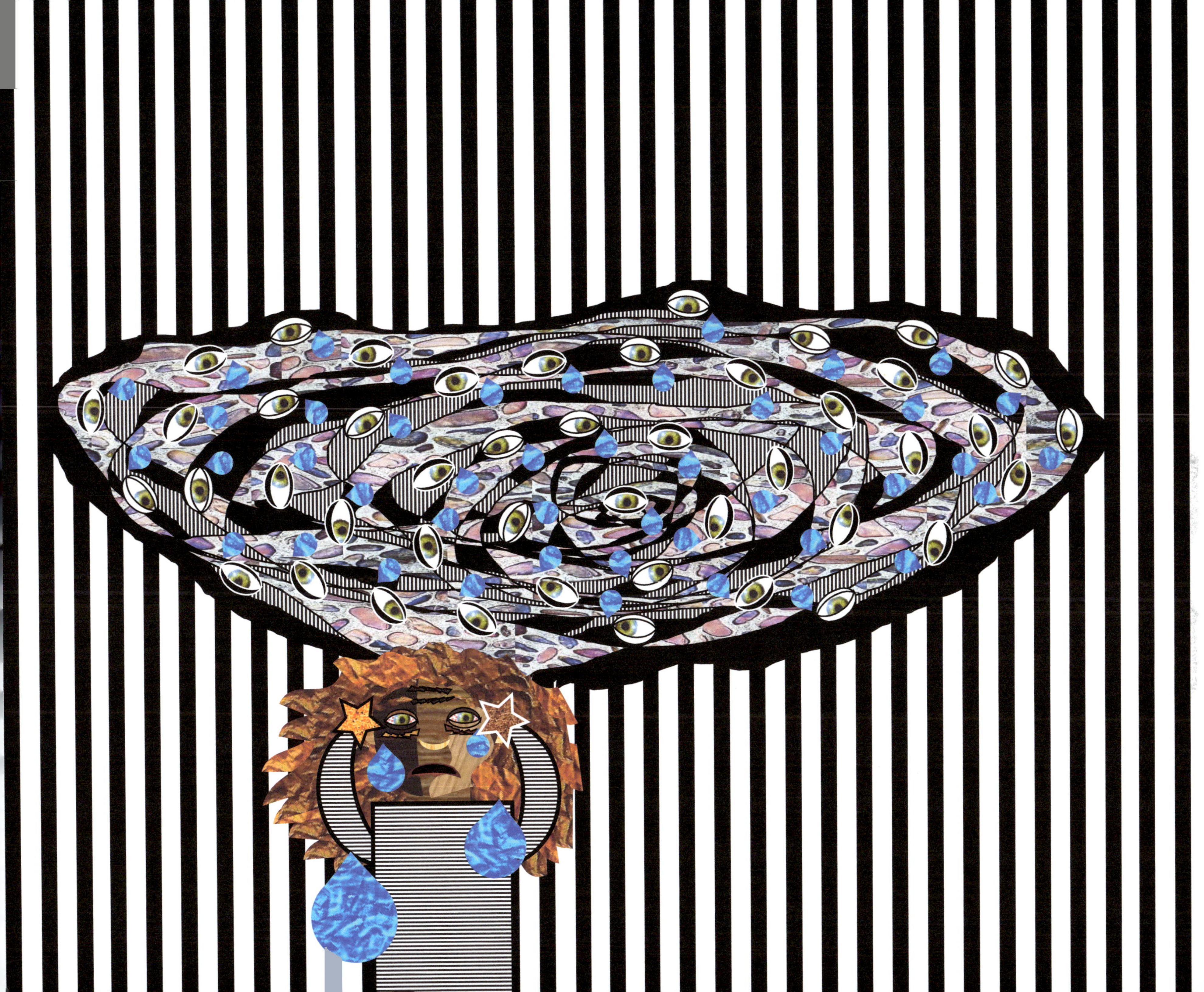

"If you ever lose hope,"
another Survivor had told her,
"and cannot find it by looking,
feel it by doing."

Earth to till,
seeds to plant,
fields to wander,
forests to explore,
seas to swim,
people to embrace,
animals to caress,
conversations and community,
books and butterflies,
flowers and fireflies,
and all the tools she used to extract
MAGIC
from her spirit and
transform her wonder into a tangible
REALITY
existed

on the other side of the walls.

What could she do?

HO PE

"If you ever lose hope,"
another Survivor had told her,
"and do not know what to do,
do what you can."

She surveyed the wall again.
It repeated,

"I CANNOT BE CLIMBED."

"However,"
the cement said, raising its voice,
"the wall can be broken.
Scratch."

She did.
Dust.

Little by little, haze filled the air.
She scratched

until her nails
cracked and her skin split open;

until bleeding
was a companion to breathing;

until her fingers
lost the memory of stillness;

until pain
became an expectation;

until exhaustion
overwhelmed her.

Then purpose overpowered exhaustion,
and she kept working

until

one stone,
as dusty as the desert,
as unsteady as the sea,
instructed her,
"Push."

She did, and her fingers
afforded her eyes a small hole:
a view to the other side.

She looked.

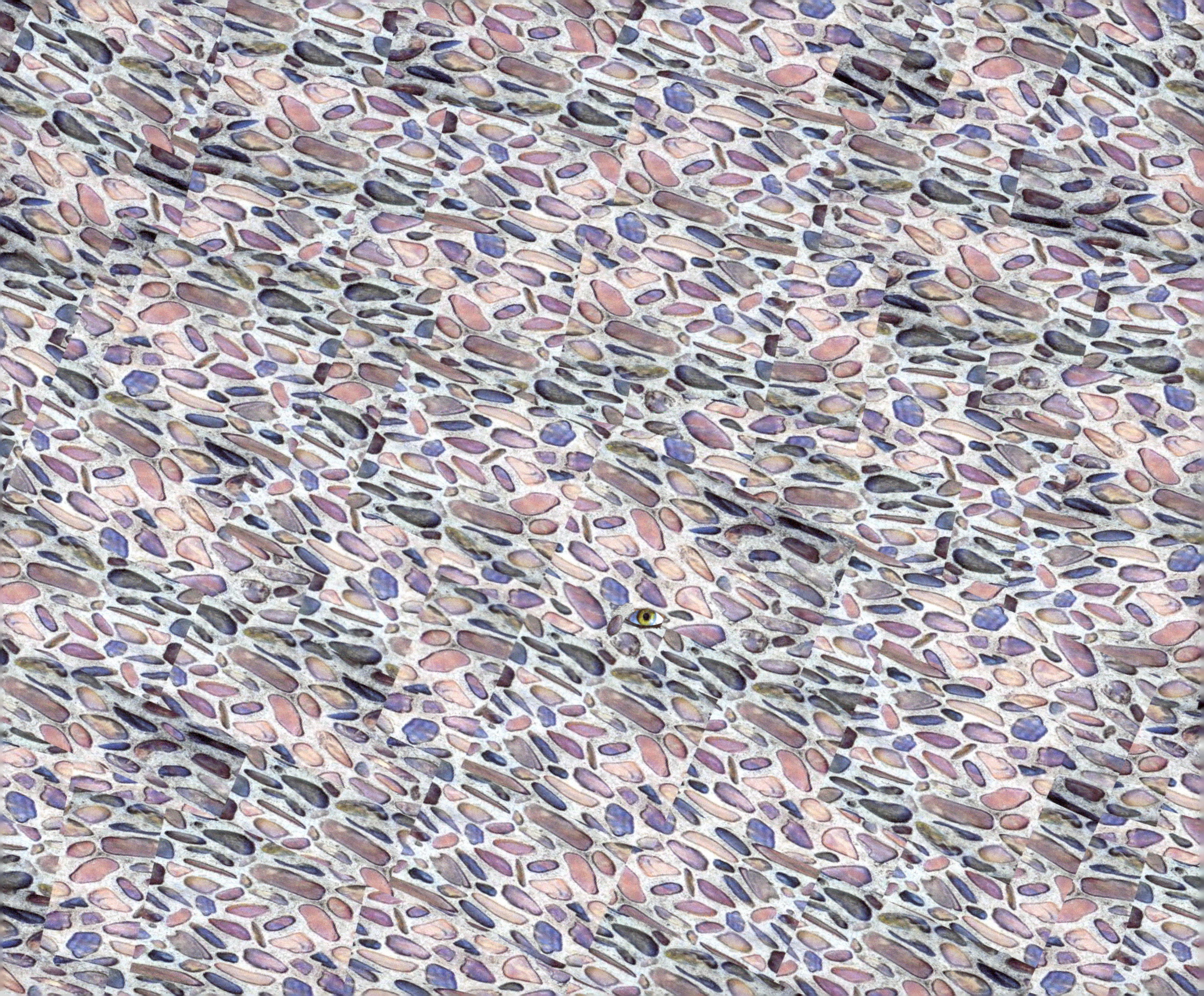

Darkness.

Her eyes closed.

Her resolve left her.

The exhaustion that purpose had staved off returned
and this time,

it triumphed.

Five words emerged from her lips
before sleep granted a reprieve from pain:

“Do
not
let
me
awaken.”

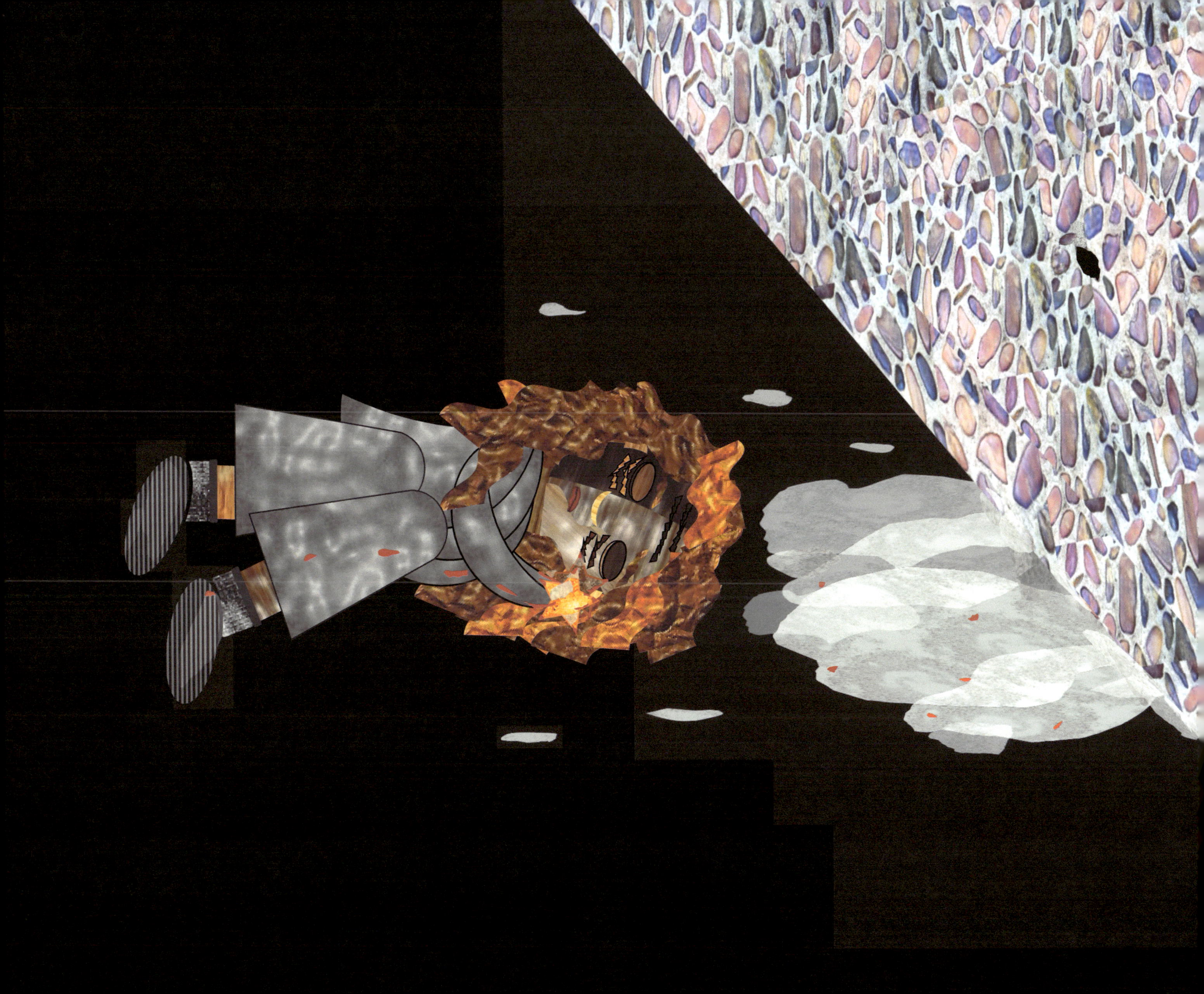

Yet awaken she did,
and the words in her heart
when she opened her eyes...

...were from one more Survivor.

"If you ever lose hope,
don't just do what you can.
Do it again.

And then again.

And again.

And again.

And again."

She rose.
Not with hope,
but with trust in the Survivors,
for if *they* insisted that she carry on,
there must be a reason why.

She returned to the wall
and continued to scratch.

Cracked nails
tore.

Skin
split anew.

Every wound
bore another wound.

Sweat drenched her and
dust piled up at her feet.

Another stone insisted, "Push."
Another offering from her
hands to her eyes.

She peered again through the hole.

Gleaming in the night sky was a single star.

She scratched more;
pushed harder.

A second star shone,
its beams steady and strong.

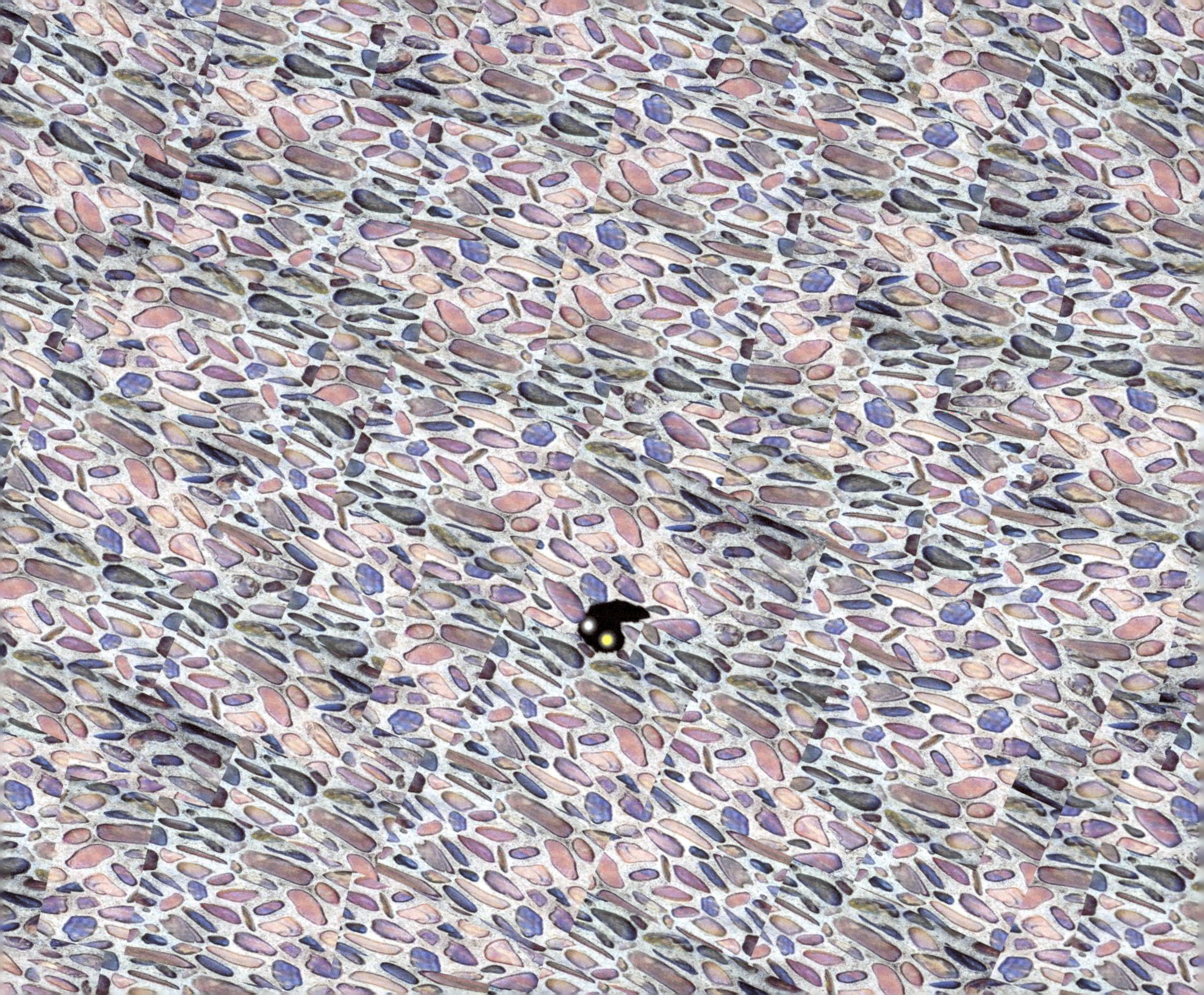

She tugged, tore.

Moonlight reached her.

She clawed;

crumbled despair's
power to powder,

and cleared the remains
from her path.

She made a door and...

...stepped through to the other side.

Kindness sang,

"What has been
will always be."

Joy poured laughter into the sky before explaining to her,
in a voice as warm as the sun,

"Silenced does not mean gone.
I have never left you
and never will."

Love

bloomed gardens around her and within her,
   sowed seeds and reaped flowers' scents at the selfsame time,
   transformed giving and receiving into synonyms,
    and serenaded every root and bud and blossom with:

"Grow.
Grow.
Grow."

The Survivors breathed a collective sigh of relief.

They abandoned their "ifs" and spoke their "whens."

"When hope returns,
and it will because it can,
listen to it."

"When hope returns,
and it will because it must,
nurture it."

"When hope returns,
and it will because it will,
share it."

She spoke her "if."

"If you ever lose hope,
think of the Survivors.
For what *they* have done,
you can do."

HO PE

LO
V
E

LOVE
WINS